THE PATIO
CLUB®

WRITTEN AND ILLUSTRATED BY

CARYN MOTTILLA

The
January Jackpot

The January Jackpot
The Patio Club®
Published by Open Window Publishing
Castle Rock, CO

Publisher's Cataloging-in-Publication data

Names: Mottilla, Caryn, author.
Title: The January Jackpot / by Caryn Mottilla.
Description: First trade paperback original edition. | Castle Rock [Colorado] : Open Window Publishing.
Identifiers: ISBN 978-0-9997471-2-4
Subjects: LCSH: Old age—Fiction. | Jackpot—Fiction. | Short stories.
BISAC: FICTION / General.
Classification: LCC PS374.O43 | DDC 813–dc22

Cover design by Caryn Mottilla

QUANTITY PURCHASES: Schools, companies, professional groups, clubs, and other organizations may qualify for special terms when ordering quantities of this title. For information, email ThePatioClub@gmail.com.

OPEN WINDOW
PUBLISHING

The Patio Club® is dedicated to the men and women in assisted living communities, memory and Hospice care who have listened to the adventures of The Patio Club®. They expressed their hope for these stories to be published and shared with others across the country.

An Introduction to The Patio Club

The Patio Club was originally formed by two sets of sisters— Elaine and Adele from New Jersey, and Betty and Mildred from Kentucky. The women were young when they met in the 1940s. The years passed by, and later in life, the four adventurous women made a pact that after they died they would meet up and visit retirement and assisted living communities. After they passed away, they came to Happy Visions Retirement Home and liked it so much they decided to stay.

The women call themselves "The Patio Club," because they sit outside on the patio of Happy Visions. Each day, Elaine, Adele,

Betty and Mildred are surrounded by colorful sparkles, and they meet a steady stream of interesting visitors and residents who pass through Happy Visions on their way to unknown destinations.

One amazing thing is that the Patio Club can look to the sky and watch a video of each person's life. This precious gift lets the Patio Club understand the unique story that each person carries with them.

The January Jackpot

IT WAS MID-JANUARY, AND ALL OF THE HOLIDAY decorations had been taken down by the staff at Happy Visions Retirement Home. Snowmen decorations still appeared on shelves and over the fireplace as a reminder that winter was still in full swing.

Outside, snow flurries and cloudy skies painted January a dreary gray. Sharp winds dropped the windchill to a frosty five degrees below zero. The spirits of the staff and residents seemed to match the quiet of the frozen first month of the year.

Inside of Happy Visions, Mildred was walking in the hallway. She was the first one in the Patio Club to notice an odd-looking coin rolling along the first-floor hallway. Elaine, Adele and Betty looked and suddenly realized what Mildred was seeing.

Walter the dog had been napping on a worn plaid blanket in the corner, and he lifted his head and watched as the old coin soundlessly passed by him. Walter did not seem to have a lot of energy these days. Months ago, he would have chased the coin and maybe even tried to eat it!

For the past week, the only excitement for the residents was the rumor that someone new was coming to Happy Visions. Gossip was circulating saying the newest resident was a man who had won a very large lottery.

When the residents began speaking about the man— Elaine, Adele, Betty and Mildred decided not to waste time with rumors. Instead, they went outside and looked up to the dark gray January sky, knowing they could watch a

video that would tell them the story of who was coming.

When the four women looked up to the sky, instead of seeing the video, they saw several crows flying overhead obstructing the view of the video as it began to play. The flapping of the crows' wings sounded like cotton sheets being shaken before being hung on a line to dry.

After the crows passed, the January sky suddenly revealed a dark, grainy video of a short, heavy-set man standing in front of TV cameras. The man was holding a large check that read, "$100 Million Dollars".

"Good heavens!" said Adele. "The newest resident won $100 million dollars! Why would someone who won $100 million dollars come to Happy Visions Retirement Home?"

Elaine chimed in and said, "He could buy a ticket and go anywhere in the world. Why on earth would he come here?"

Emerald green sparkles surrounded the women of the Patio Club as they looked at the video in the sky. The

women were like detectives and sensed that something seemed strange. In the video, the man stood all alone as he hugged an over-sized replica of a check. He had a nervous smile on his face. No friends or family were anywhere in sight. The man looked around cautiously as though he were afraid that someone would take the check if he let go of it.

As the video continued, the television people asked the man how he would spend the money. The man smirked and said, "I am going to keep it all for myself." Then he laughed. He said he felt that Life owed him something because he had never had a break. It was finally his turn for the best things that money could buy!

Now, you might imagine that the TV people would be happy for this man. However, that was not the case. As the TV people watched him, they felt sorry for him and shook their heads and turned the cameras off. The man was left standing all alone on the stage. He seemed not to notice that everyone had walked away.

Elaine, Adele, Mildred and Betty looked sad as they watched the video. They knew that the man would have a story to tell when he arrived. After the video in the sky stopped playing, the women straightened the chairs on the patio and went back inside.

That was when Mildred again noticed the strange coin rolling on the linoleum floor in the hallway that led to the living room. Sparkles swirled behind Mildred as she ran after the coin. When she stomped her foot to stop the coin from rolling, a burst of brilliant purple light lit up the hallway, and Mildred yelled with surprise!

"What was that!" cried Elaine. "Did you see that? That looked like lightening." Walter the dog barked when he saw the burst of brilliant purple light. He walked the fastest he had in weeks and went into the living room to hide under a sofa.

"Wait a minute," said Betty. "Let's think about this. It has to be a trick coin of some kind." They would know the answer in a minute because the coin was now under

Mildred's shoe. Mildred moved her foot, and picked up the coin to look at it. The face of the coin had a picture of a man she did not recognize. She turned the coin over and read the inscription on the back to the others:

"Only a change of heart will free you
from the burden of this money.
To those who cling to it,
Loneliness will follow like a shadow."

The women of the Patio Club looked at each other. Elaine had worked at a bank. She said, "I remember people that guarded their money and never spent it. They lived each day afraid that they were going to lose it. They seldom seemed happy."

Adele was the next to speak. "People like that are more focused on money than they are on the riches of Life. It is sad in a way. They miss so much."

Betty said, "I wish I had that problem. The only large sum of money I ever received was when I was in a car

accident. Maybe large sums of money bring more trouble than they are worth."

Mildred now stood holding the coin. She spoke softly as she said, "I secretly wished my whole life to win a lot of money. I often thought it would bring me more happiness. Looking back now, I realize that I was always happy with what I actually had."

About that time, the front door to Happy Visions suddenly blew open. A moment later, an older gentleman walked inside, pulling a black suitcase and carrying a large, green duffel bag. He removed his cap, and looked around. His brown boots were old and worn with holes in the leather. The man looked lost and that was when Marilyn, one of the residents, walked up to the stranger and said hello.

Marilyn kindly welcomed the man and asked if she could help him. "Today is my first day here," he said. "I am afraid I do not know where to go." Marilyn's kindness seemed touch the man in a special way. A smile crossed his face as he began to follow Marilyn to the office.

The women of the Patio Club watched the couple and noticed that the man had several purple sparkles trailing behind him. In fact, the purple sparkles were the same color as the burst of purple light that came from the rolling coin when Mildred stepped on it!

"Let me see that coin," said Betty. As Mildred handed it to her, she noticed that the coin was warm. Betty looked with wonder at the front of the old and unusual coin. Suddenly Betty said, "The face on the front of the coin looks exactly like the man that just walked through the door. It's HIM!" cried Betty. "In fact, it's the man we saw in the video too!"

Betty turned the old, discolored coin over her in hand and again read the inscription out loud:

"Only a change of heart will free you
from the burden of this money.
To those who cling to it,
Loneliness will follow like a shadow."

"It is almost like a curse," said Betty, "A curse that only love and friendship can break."

Elaine, Adele, Betty and Mildred were surprised by Marilyn's attentiveness to the newest arrival. Since arriving at Happy Visions in October, Marilyn's memory failed her more each day. Walter the dog now seemed new to her every time she saw him.

The Patio Club noticed when Marilyn greeted the older gentleman at the door, she looked excited. In fact, it seemed as though she already knew him. What no one, including Marilyn, knew was that the newest resident had been the only boyfriend Marilyn ever had. They broke up after high school when he went in search of his dream of making millions.

Earlier in the day, the residents held a contest to guess how much money the millionaire had won. After dinner, they announced the winner. They decided to let Marilyn win the prize, which was choosing the movie the residents would watch that evening. They also gave Marilyn the $5

in the jackpot.

Residents went into the living room to watch the movie that Marilyn picked, and the newest resident was with them. The millionaire's name was Max. He sat on a couch near the fireplace, and Marilyn sat next to him. She seemed more alert than she had in weeks.

During the movie, the women of the Patio Club noticed that Max spoke quietly to Marilyn. At one point, they saw Max lean over and ask Marilyn, "Do you remember this movie? It was one of our favorites?" Marilyn's eyes widened as she pondered Max's question, and a smile crossed her face.

The Patio Club was getting excited. It was the feeling they felt when something extraordinary was going to happen. Elaine said, "I think Marilyn recognizes Max from her past. Let's go watch the video in the sky."

The women did not feel the frigid air as they entered the patio and looked to the sky. This time the video showed

two lovers in high school. The young couple walked home after school holding hands. In the summer, they walked to a park and later that day saw a movie. Suddenly, the women of the Patio Club realized that it was a young Max and Marilyn.

The video continued as Max waved goodbye to Marilyn as he set out on his journey of making millions. During the years that followed, Max made some money trying several get-rich-quick schemes, but it was never enough. He carried all his money in a green duffel bag. His only focus his entire life had been holding on to the bag and the money it contained.

Max's life was about chasing money instead of relationships and love. He suffered the loneliness that comes when money is more important than friendship, love or community.

Marilyn sat waiting for Max to return. She lived alone with her cat in a house on the outskirts of the town where they grew up. She spent most of her life waiting for Max

while she read about the adventures that other people take. She also lost out on real relationships and love as she waited for Max.

...But love has a way of reuniting those who seem most lost...

Residents noticed that Max left his large, green duffel bag at the front door when he arrived. He never unpacked the money it contained. He had an easy way about him now, and he smiled as he talked to the residents that he sat with each day. His true riches were now in his heart.

Mildred now carried the coin that she had found rolling in the hallway. Each day the coin slowly lost more of its warmth. The purple burst of color was never seen again. The sparkles that followed Max were no longer purple. Now they were like the colors of the rainbow. It reminded the Patio Club of the jackpot that is rumored to be at the end of each rainbow. Maybe Max had finally found his jackpot.

All stories come with a moral, and in this case, there are a few. For Marilyn, she hit the jackpot she hoped for—the dream that Max would return someday. Even though her memory no longer works, her heart surely recognizes him.

For Max, the emptiness that comes when you realize that money cannot fill your heart will humble even the strongest people. Max finally hit the jackpot he hoped for his entire life. It's the feeling that comes from the joy and delight of connecting with others. If only the TV people could interview him now.

Later that day, the Patio Club talked about what they had witnessed. The coin had lost its warmth. Elaine, Adele, Mildred and Betty had held it in their hands. Each of them had seen the picture of Max on the front of the coin and read the inscription on the back.

As the Patio Club went one last time in the late January afternoon to look to the sky and the video that played, they saw doves flying soundlessly overhead. The video now showed the old coin. Max's picture was gone from the front of it, and in its place, was a couple who held hands with a brilliant sun shining behind them. The new inscription on the back of the coin now read:

True wealth

is measured by the love

that one accumulates and shares

over the course of

a lifetime...

As Mildred looked at the coin she held in her hand, she realized that it had indeed been transformed—the way Love can do at just the right time. With love, it is never too late to hit the jackpot!

Good luck from the Patio Club!

The Patio Club's Story

IN NOVEMBER OF 2016, I began writing fictional stories for retirement and assisted living communities. This occurred because of a simple request from an older gentleman in his 80s who asked if I could write a story about people "their age." Writing and telling stories has always come easily to me. I happily said , "yes." I was excited at the challenge and have written a story each month since then. They are about a fictional retirement/ assisted living community named *Happy Visions*. Each month I read to retirement and assisted living communities. The joy of doing this is overwhelming.

In July of 2017, I was reading to a group of older women as they sat outside *on the patio* in the shade. The women's ages reached up to 95. When I left the patio that day, I decided at that moment to write a story for them called "The Patio Club." The series began with that story.

The stories I write come effortlessly to me. It is as if I am divinely inspired. As I began writing the first story in the Patio Club series, I was so surprised as I watched the story come to life. It is the story of two sets of sisters, Elaine and Adele from New Jersey, and Mildred and Betty from Kentucky. They made a pact that when they died they would meet up and visit retirement and assisted living communities.

Imagine my surprise—because in real life Elaine and Adele (sisters) were my aunts from New Jersey, and Betty (my mother) and Mildred (my aunt) were sisters from Kentucky! My Aunt Mildred was the last one to join The Patio Club. She passed away earlier in 2017. The Patio Club™ stories now touch people from around the country and hopefully someday from around the world.

My dream is that The Patio Club™ series will be read to the people in assisted living, memory and Hospice care communities. As I read each month to these special people, I realized that it is often difficult to visit loved ones who are in the assisted living population. What I have found is that reading a story seems to transform everyone from the reader to the listener. I have seen people with all kinds of health challenges perk up when listening to the joyful adventures of The Patio Club™. They are in the present moment as they listen and during that time there is nothing wrong with them.

My wish is that people will take the adventure of reading a story (about 12 to 15 minutes) from The Patio Club Series to a loved one. It will transform the visit from one where it may be difficult to find something to talk about, to one where both the reader and listener are moved beyond words.

With gratitude and love,

- Caryn

Acknowledgments

THE PATIO CLUB is dedicated to my aunts Elaine, Adele, Mildred, and my mother Betty. Although the characters in the Patio Club are fictional, they are based on these important women who impacted my life.

Special thanks to my sons Carson and Cooper, as well as, family and friends who have listened to these stories. They have enthusiastically cheered for me to follow my dream to write and illustrate stories that bring joy and adventure to the lives of others.

Finally, I am grateful to God for the gifts He has given me to serve the people in assisted living, memory and Hospice care.

About the Author

CARYN BEGAN WRITING children's stories for her children in the 1990s. In 2016, as she read children's stories to assisted living communities, residents asked her to write a story "for people their age." That was how the adventure of writing for the adult and assisted population began.

Since that time, Caryn has written a monthly series called The Patio Club®. It takes place at a retirement home/assisted living community named Happy

Visions. The Patio Club™ are the first stories published by Caryn for that age group. The stories have captured the attention of people of all ages across the country.

The Patio Club™ stories are a bridge between the reader and the listener. Family and friends that visit assisted living, memory and Hospice care communities may struggle for something to talk about. Reading a story like The Patio Club™ to these special residents takes them on an adventure without them ever having to leave the room. It creates an opening for some interesting conversations!

Caryn lives in Colorado. She has two grown sons, Carson and Cooper

www.ingramcontent.com/pod-product-compliance
Lightning Source LLC
Chambersburg PA
CBHW080019130626
46556CB00016B/3307